Bassoon
Sight-reading

from 2018

ABRSM Grades 1–5

Contents

First published in 2017 by ABRSM (Publishing) Ltd, a wholly owned subsidiary of ABRSM
© 2017 by The Associated Board of the Royal Schools of Music
Unauthorized photocopying is illegal

Music origination by Moira Roach
Cover by Kate Benjamin & Andy Potts
Printed in England by Halstan & Co. Ltd, Amersham, Bucks., on materials from sustainable sources

Grade 1

Grade 1

Grade 2

Grade 2

Lullaby

13

Alla marcia

14

Espressivo

15

Allegretto

16

Grade 2

Grade 3

Grade 3

Grade 3

Grade 4

Grade 4

Grade 4

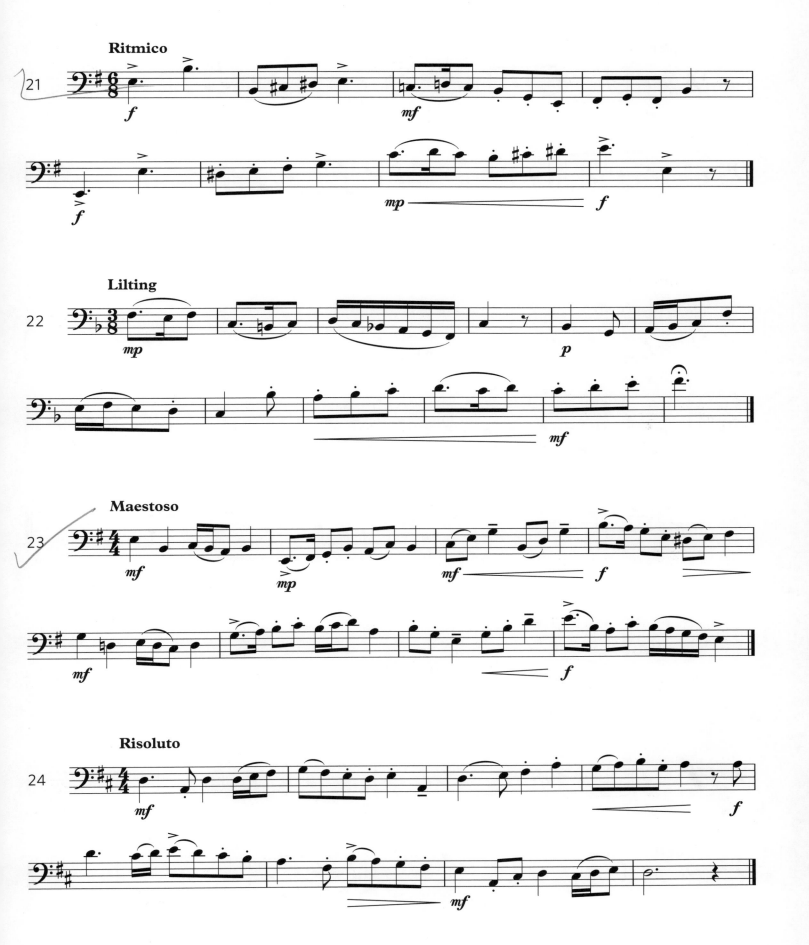

Grade 5

Vivace

4

Marziale

5

Misterioso

6

26

Grade 5

Grade 5

13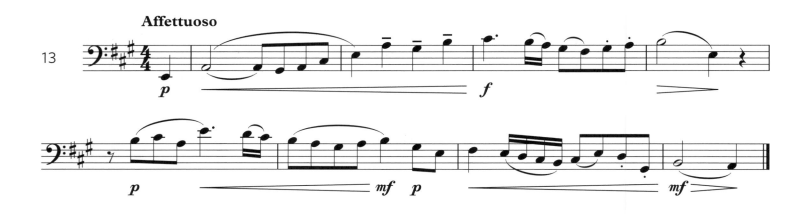

14

15

Grade 5

Cantando

19

Con brio

20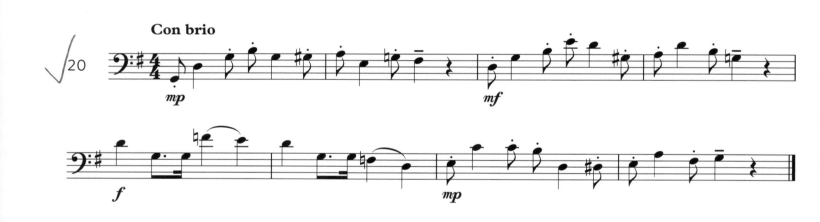

Vivo

21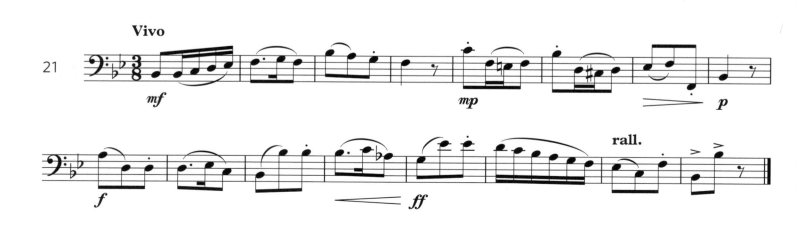

Bassoon Sight-reading

This book contains valuable practice material for candidates preparing for ABRSM's Bassoon exams at Grades 1–5. It features sample sight-reading tests for the new requirements from 2018, written in attractive and approachable styles.

Also available:

 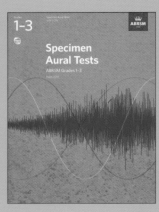 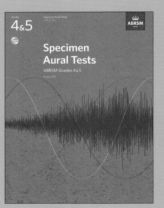

Digital resources are also available from the ABRSM app centre: www.abrsm.org/appcentre.

Aural Trainer   Speedshifter

Supporting the teaching and learning of music in partnership with the Royal Schools of Music

Royal Academy of Music | Royal College of Music
Royal Northern College of Music | Royal Conservatoire of Scotland

www.abrsm.org   f facebook.com/abrsm
🐦 @abrsm   ▶ ABRSM YouTube

ISBN 978-1-84849-975-1

9 781848 499751

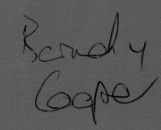

Bassoon
Scales & Arpeggios

from 2018
ABRSM Grades 1–5

Learning scales and arpeggios helps you to develop reliable muscle-memory for common finger movements, and to improve your tone control across the full note range. It also helps you to develop your pitch and interval awareness, and to become familiar with keys and their related patterns.

You can find a complete list of scales and arpeggios required for Grades 1–5 in the back of this book. In the exam, they should be played from memory. The given metronome marks are for guidance only. Slurred requirements should be legato throughout. Choosing where to breathe is left to your discretion but breaths should disturb the flow as little as possible.

These requirements are valid from 1 January 2018. Reference must always be made to the syllabus for the year in which the exam is to be taken, in case any changes have been made to the requirements.
www.abrsm.org/woodwind